# Kitty K.

## Liz Crowe

Interior design and layout by Crowerotica Fantasies.

Cover design by NML Book Cover Design.

Kitty K.

## Chapter One

I CAN FEEL THE EYES of the bellboy pierce through me as I walk off with my 'prize find'. We're heading to the elevator and if at least I can believe what he whispered into my ears minutes earlier.

*"We should go to my penthouse on the top floor."*

He nods as we arrive at the elevator. I can see my own reflection in the bronzed doors, and I smile alluringly at him as I feel his hand take hold of my ass. I don't mind. It's why I decided to let him chat me up in the first place in the bar next to the hotel.

I stare teasingly at the bellboy when I turn in the elevator.

*Your turn will come later. I don't mind some virgin territory to pass my time.*

He nods to the row of buttons, and I lean forward to press the top button. It's red. Just my kind of colour. As the door close, I feel him press against my ass; his hand sliding up under my top. He doesn't wait long to give me the entertainment I yearn for. As his hand slides up I feel my blouse move ever so slowly over my nipples that react to three things: the cool air rising up under my blouse, his hand reaching for my right nipple and the wonderful feeling of him pushing himself hard against my ass. I'm so ready for what's to come that I can feel the juices damping my pants.

*How* he manages to slide my jeans and pants down over my hips, is going to be a mystery to solve later. I'd never met any guy *yet*, who could do it so effortlessly. I lean forward further, so as to allow him full access. He's inside me before I know it. I curve my back to do one other thing, while he gives me my entertainment.
Looking up at the tiny black box to my left at

the top of the elevator, I know who's likely watching me there. It's quite likely the bellboy is now sitting in that tiny room behind the check-in desk, jerking off while he watching *him* ramming me like it's the end of the world.

I moan when the first effects of the entertainment heighten my own arousal…

~~~

The doors glide open just as I reach the third orgasm, and to my surprise, I'm hoisted into his arms before I can even move my ass away from him. This short trek from the elevator is an interesting new experience for me. One arm, rippling with well-shaped muscles, lifts me from the floor of the lift; his other arm decides to embrace me by cupping my left boob. Having his hot hand over my cold boob increases my expectations of what's to come next.

Still riding his dick, we 'walk' to a massive door. My eyes fly open when we *do* arrive in an exquisitely decorated penthouse. It's huge. It causes me to squeeze my pussy tight over his cock which is still inside me. As I squeeze tight, it decides to stop deep in my moist well.
~~~

"Do you like what you see?" he murmurs into my ear.

I let out a gasp of exaltation as he pushes once more deep inside, before slowly lowering me to the floor.

I feel disappointment when he pulls out, and I turn to look at him. I smile alluringly at him as a way to encourage him. I wait for his next actions.
"Would you like to have champagne?"
I nod.
I'm not really into drinking alcohol, but I'm certain *this* penthouse comes with expensive champagne.
"I'll shower first, then I'll retrieve a bottle to share. Make yourself comfortable on the sofa."

I glance quickly over my shoulder when he nods to somewhere behind me. I smile when I spot the massive sofa. I think I could fit a bus full of my girlfriends on it and *still* have space to spread out myself. I smirk at the idea of offering an orgy to my prize find…

When I turn I'm alone.
I look around quickly and just catch him walking around the corner taking off his shirt. I

draw in my breath when I see the 'hunk' underneath the clothing.

"He said shower…" I mumble, and my words cause my feet to start walking. *Not* to the sofa, he offered, but in the same direction as the hunk had gone.

If he was showering it would mean I could entertain myself in yet another way.

He turns, looking somewhat surprised to see me standing at the doorway to the bathroom. I grin when I realise that a penthouse doesn't come with a bathroom door to lock.

It only takes me moments for my blouse, jeans and pants to lie on the floor in a pile…next to his clothing. When I look up I'm met with a knowing grin…

# Chapter Two

Hot water splashes over my head, turning my head up towards it, opening my mouth. He leans in against my body. I feel his hands, each slick with shower gel, slide slowly over my boobs. Somehow, his hands feel even hotter than before.

I draw in my breath as his left hand decides to play a little game. It decides to take hold of my boob, massage it, flick my nipple ever so slowly, then it starts on a journey down. Every place where it touches my skin, I feel a sensation soar through my entire body.

# Kitty K.



*I want him to fuck me like he did in the elevator.*

Normally, I'm quite reserved in how much I want to do with my prize finds, but with *this* hunk, it seems different. He makes me hunger for him. He needs to take me. Now!

I moan when he pushes his finger against my clit. I feel surprised when his finger finds a hard knob. His finger slides inside. Deep, gloriously, and hot.

"You have a hot pussy," he whispers in my ear.

His hard rod pushes against my ass as an answer when a moan escapes my mouth.

"Do you want to play?" he whispers.

I think I nodded because somehow I slid around. He kisses my mouth passionately, but then I'm on my knees in front of him.

I don't pause when I see his dick in front of my face. I grab hold of it with my hand. Somehow, it's covered in shower gel. My hand glides over his hard-on with such ease that I start smiling with delight. This is the sort of game I can enjoy…

~~~

I look up after I've managed to make him moan for the third time in under ten minutes.

"Did you like that?" I ask him.

He nods, grinning at me again with that magnetism he had used in the bar to convince me to go with him.

His hands lift me to my feet and he pins me against the wall. I might as well be on fire when he starts kissing me passionately on every place of my naked skin. His right-hand caresses my mound, sending surges of spasms through my body.

He leans over and takes one of my nipples in his mouth, pulling on it teasingly with his teeth. I guess he's experienced in this teasing as the action heightens my own expectations for what will come once he carries me to the sofa…or the bed perhaps. He nibbles my other nipple, flicking his tongue against it. The combination of the hot water splashing down and him flicking causes me to feel like I need him to fuck me. I decide on a new approach.
~~~

"Fuck me hard," I whisper. The playful nibbles stop, and when I open my eyes I'm staring into his lusting eyes.

His hand, which had been playing with my mound lowers, and three of his fingers enter my well forcefully. But the feeling causes a loud groan to escape from my mouth.
"I can fuck you in many ways," he swoons at me.
"Please…do it all to me. I'm so ready for it."
At least I *think* I said that.

His right hand now moves in and out of my well. He has an answer, even if I never spoke. I think he can see on my face how much I want this. I moan now each time his fingers go inside. I don't want him to stop.

~~~

I have no idea how I ended up on the bed. *How* he managed to carry me from the shower to the bed, while still busy entertaining my deep well with his three fingers. It has to be cold in the bedroom, but I'm feeling *so* hot it doesn't matter. We could easily be in the middle of the arctic or a
~~~

desert, and I'd only feel the heat coming from deep inside me as I'm turned on more and more by every motion of his fingers or his kisses over my cold skin.

"I want you to take me…please…" I manage to call out between the moans. It results in his fingers pause their motion while his thumb plays with my knob. I feel him beside me and I reach around it causes my hand to take hold of his cock in my hand. My hand decides it wants to play its own game with him. It seems to have an effect on him because he starts moaning, too. Each motion from me causes him to become faster with the motions of his hand.

"Take me…" I moan. It's all I can utter when another massive orgasm surges through my body. A deliriously glorious orgasm of a magnitude I've never experienced before. And I've experienced a few over the years. But none equal the one this man manages to exert from my body.

And *this* is just the foreplay…

## Chapter Three

WE PAUSE A WHILE FOR him to get the champagne he had promised me. We sip from a single glass, leaning side by side - both naked for convenience - in the bed. Part of me has to admit that the bed is a better choice.

*I wonder if all my girlfriends would fit on this bed for the orgy.*

I smile at the idea even though I know most of them aren't into 'my stuff'.
"What's the happy smile for?"
"I was just enjoying the thought of more…"

Okay, that wasn't really what I thought about, but I decided a long time ago that any prize finds were not for sharing. Especially this one.

"I guess you're still not going to tell me your name."

"Kitty…"

"Perfect name for a *hot* babe with a *hot* pussy."

I smile at him before I sip some champagne; it's the really expensive stuff which I'm pretty sure is sold for a hundred bucks or more by the glass in the most expensive restaurants. I don't know, but it sure *does* taste expensive.

*Don't get cocky with yourself, Kitty, you know you'll be gone in hours from now. Just play along, and let him entertain you…*

I glance at the bulge in the bed sheet. I know his cock is flaccid right now. I guess it's gathering strength for round *two*: the full-on sex that's to come.

What had so far was just the foreplay. I feel satisfaction to have had him fuck me at least once, and for him to have entertained me so much that I have had a least thirty minutes of my boredom filled. He was not going to be the first or last to entertain me.

He came with a room full of more entertainment. I had my pick…

~~~

I feel hot breath near my ear. His lips kiss my neck a moment later. He'd downed six glasses of the champagne so far, and his breath smelled of alcohol. I guess his drunken mind is making him horny again. Or perhaps it's my hand motions. My hand speeds up. The flaccid state of his cock starts to lessen a few minutes later much to my delight. I smile at him, and I'm greeted with a big, boyish smirk. He knows what I'm doing to him. He just has to wait just that little bit longer before he can take me.

His hand caresses over my belly. It causes a renewed feeling of electricity soaring through my body. It feels like he's rubbing a blown-up balloon over my skin.

For a few moments, his hand decides to rest over my boobs with my nipples standing up to attention. He leans over and flicks his tongue over the nearest boob. I can see my other nipple harden and become even firmer as he plays his tongue over the one nearest to him. It doesn't take
~~~

long before the first moan escapes his mouth, and that's the cue for his right hand to travel down over my skin. It glides so softly over my skin that I get goosebumps in places. But the feelings triggered from that just add to the ever-growing lusting I start to feel for him to be inside me with his massive rod.

My hand slides slowly up, feeling the hardness of the rod. At the top, it meets the precum oozing from the tip. My finger plays with the sticky juice. I manage to surprise him because he lets out a loud moan.

But when his fingers reach my mound, I pause my actions. When I pause, so does he. It becomes a new game…

His fingers reach my deep well, and suddenly it doesn't matter if don't keep playing. His fingers entering inside me, have me gasping and grabbing at the bedding. I moan loudly, "More…please…take me…"

Each time his finger moves over my knob, he stops for a moment, seemingly to tease me with a heightened anticipation. I don't mind it. I'm so turned on now that he might as well ram his cock right inside me, and ravage me for many hours until the sunlight streams through the massive windows of the penthouse.

"Kitty…"

My name escapes his mouth as a moan. I realise that my hand had decided to continue with its earlier game of tease. I guess the reason for the moan was me doing that…

"Your skin tastes so sweet," he murmurs.

"Every part of me tastes sweet…" I whisper.

He looks up, and his face cracks into a mischievous smile. "I guess that was an invitation to taste," he says.

I nod.

"You want me to taste…"

I nod again. I'm about to answer but I realise it wasn't a question.

He moves away slowly from me, constantly smiling. A moment later his hard rod is out of my reach.

He smiles at me once more as he pushes my legs apart….

## Chapter Four

HIS HANDS SLOWLY CARESS THE insides of my thighs and even though I had my earlier experiences with the guys I'd seduce, this guy's effort is new for me.

He knows precisely where to touch me; the right pressure, the right places for his fingers, the right speed, everything is just so perfect about how he's preparing this next game with me.

My senses, even some imagined senses that only ever seem to appear whenever I'd find myself naked in a bed with a guy, are all on high alert.

They all want what's coming next.

His hands are over my hips a moment later, and unexpectedly I'm pulled flat on the bed…closer to his face, closer to his tongue that wants to play its own new game.

The initial touch from his tongue against my clit is so tender yet able to touch me in that very specific spot on my clit that I'm left gasping as much as I did before. Again it comes. It causes my body to arch. An arm pushes under my body before I can relax. Touch comes again.

I moan loudly.

His other hand caresses over my belly, slowly moving up to my boob until his hand reaches my nipple once more. His finger flicks my nipple. For a few moments I feel disappointment, but then, unexpectedly his tongue plunges into my pussy.

I gasp.

His tongue feels so hot against my flower petals he must be tasting with delight. I feel his arm push me up and because of this, his tongue digs deeper for my juices.

I groan loud, "Ooh…that…feels…good."

His hand squeezes my boob, then just as I reach another peak, the tongue is gone. My anticipated next peak deflates with the denial of the continued game. But then I sense movement. I hold my breath and dare not open my eyes. As he towers over me, he kisses my lips once more.

My eyes open when the next motion results with him deep inside me. He grins at the obvious surprise that's now visible on my face. He pulls back, then rams deep once more. He honours me by slowly sliding away and repeating the thrust with added force.

The sensations are so different from every other time. Every time he pushes in, he heightens my sensations. Before I know it I'm moaning loud continuously and grasping at the bed sheets. I feel my body arch up when another wave of orgasms ripples through my body. My body arching obviously is an invitation for him to lean forward and he sucks on my right nipple. I draw my breath and hold it in to let the feelings go through my mind…

"That…feels…so…good…" I whisper.

Slowly he lets go of my nipple and looks at me grinning broadly. Before I can say anything to him, he has his lips around my other nipple. I glance down at my right nipple, the cold air of the room makes it tingle. It stands to attention, tall, proud and bright pink…

"Kitty, would your pussy licked clean?"

I nod.

I feel so turned on now that it's becoming hard to speak. But before he lets me enjoy the battle between his tongue and my clit he decides to thrust his dick deep inside my pussy.

A sound that resembles a groan escapes my mouth, and then several more. As I reach the peak of my orgasm, a single thought starts to occupy my mind.

*What's next?*

He pulls out ever so slowly. The feeling it evokes causes a broad smile to emerge on my face.

"Did you enjoy that?"

I nod again, now tongue-tied because of sheer ecstasy I feel.

He moves down. As he does he plants gentle kisses on my naked skin, and each place a kiss lands my skin feels like it's on fire and each time he kisses me I moan loud. Slowly, his lips come closer to my pussy, then he reaches my mound. He stops advances and for a moment I feel like I'm going to have my second disappointment. But then his tongue caresses over my mound until reaching my clit…

Suddenly, his tongue is flicking around my clit and digging deep into my pussy with his tongue.

I become aware of my voice screaming out in pleasure at each flick of his tongue. Now my body decides to react to it with a mind of its own. I scream in ecstasy, and somehow find a way to keep telling him: "More…more… more, please…Don't stop…"

My outburst seems to make him chuckle under his breath.

I start pushing against his head with both my hands, attempting to push him away, for the sensation of my body being on fire to seize. He tightens his grip around legs; somehow he grabs hold of my hands, and he holds onto me tightly with two strong hands to force me into the most extreme orgasm I've ever experienced.

Kitty K.

25

*It feels so good….*

Chapter Five

FEELING LANGUOROUS, I LIE ON the bed, spent from the multiple times my body decide to arch from another play from his tongue. Spent and satisfied. I listen to the sound of the shower running. The second time showering this evening. I guess I can join him for some fun washing each other…

I slide off the bed slowly, and walk slowly towards the sound of splashing water is coming from. As I arrive at the shower room, I smile at him.

"I think I need washing *too*..." I say softly as I run my hand over my boobs.

"You can wash me..." he answers, pointing down. "You did a great job earlier."

He points down. I guess my appearance had a great effect on him because I stare at his dick, erect and standing to attention, pulsating like it's beckoning me closer...

"I can wash *him*. If you promise me something..." I murmur with curled up lips, showing delight at seeing his dick react to me in such an obedient way.

"Sure, go ahead..." he says.

I saunter forward at an unhurried pace. Each step I take causes his dick to pulsate and I'm certain it's somehow becoming longer. I smile at him when I reach him. He smiles broadly when my hand grabs hold of his dick. My hand slides up towards the tip of his dick.

"Is this nice...?"

I look up at him, half-smiling, waiting for an answer before I move my hand.

He nods.

My hand moves back over the slick surface of

his dick, and it decides to lift higher up and because of my intentional proximity, it decides to rub over my belly. I feel a tingle going through my pussy feeling it rub over my skin.

He groans, then closes his eyes.

My hand travels back to the tip ever so slowly. Arriving there it's met by oozing warm liquid. My finger decides to rub the tip to arouse him some more before I move my hand back down.

I grab the bottle of shower gel from the shelf behind me and proceed to comply with his wish to be washed…especially his erect dick. I stand in front of him, closing in so his dick pushes against my belly. I hold the bottle sideways so a stream of the pink liquid pours over his dick. A sharp drawing in of breath tells me that the liquid must be cold.

My hand starting moving over his dick and then softly caress his balls. The skin there is even softer and the sensation of me caressing him there seems to cause him to become aroused. His hand pushes my face up and, leaning forward, he kisses me. The new game now played, is my hand moving along his dick; his tongue probing my mouth. I have to admit he's a good kisser…

~~~

After spending thirty minutes in the shower, we decided to go back to the bed; him carrying me naked in his arms. I lean against his shoulder. Being carried this way is a first for me. He lowers me gently onto the bed, then stands to stare at me for several minutes.

"Do you realise you're beautiful..." he whispers, and the admission actually surprises me.

"I guess I am if you say it..." I comment.

"I think you are..."

He walks around the bed and lies down next to me. As soon as he lies beside me, his hand decides to caress my still wet skin once more. I can see something is on his mind. I guess I can play a different game. He starts to interest me more than I had thought possible.

His hand slowly travels down over my belly and I decided to oblige by moving my legs apart. Now his hand responds to the invitation.

I draw in my breath when he touches my clit, proving once more how ready I am for another fuck from him. And I have to admit that the fucking with him is better than anything I've
~~~

experienced to date.

"Fuck me…" I whisper. "Before I *may* need to go if they call about my plane… I want to remember this evening."

He doesn't speak and just complies by climbing on top of me, and he enters me in a single forceful thrust. He pulls out slowly, though not completely, then thrusts in hard once more, and faster.

I gasp.

His face takes on an expression of determination as he pushes inside me faster and faster. As he does, I start gasping more and more; my own orgasms start matching his. We both want this, it's obvious from how we react to the fucking that we both want.

I moan loudly as his dick decide to thrust into my pussy once more. This time, there's nothing stopping us from enjoying the sex.

"More…I want more of this…" I moan the words as another orgasm rages through my body.

# Chapter Six

T HIS TIME HE WANTS TO give me every ounce of fuck he's capable of. And I decide to lie back to let him has his way with me. No matter what my own rules are I want to have good sex with this man. He intrigues me, now more than when I was busy seducing him during the party downstairs.

I look up and see him straining with his eyes closed. I glance sideways at my cell phone wondering if I can have a few more hours of sex *before* they'll call me. Just in case, I'd muted the ringtone, and put the phone on its side so I can see the call coming in.

My attention is distracted by another thrust from him. It seems he's more and more turned on as time goes on. I guess each previous time we engaged in our game of sex - so far - it was just a way for us to give each of us as much fun as we both wanted from the current circumstances.

*But maybe he wants more from this than I do. I wonder if it relates to how aggressive he was to that other guy who tried to chat me up. I wonder if something happened to—*

My mind doesn't finish the thoughts when another hard thrust makes it scream with pleasure instead.

*He fucks so well. I wonder what his idea of us getting together again actually involves. Maybe I should ask, but in such a way that doesn't give him any ideas…*

The pause in his motions, followed by the rushes of warmth deep inside me tells that he'd cum. He doesn't pull out but instead leans sideways, and while still inside me he plays with my clit and bringing me to a new orgasm. I wonder now if most of what he's doing is to entertain me and, perhaps, to give him similar memories.

My back arches at every flick of his finger, and in the brief moment I can look at him I see a satisfied grin on his face. At the next glance in his direction, he places his lips over mine and kisses me passionately, letting his tongue probe all parts of my mouth.

At the same time, his finger increases its motions and moments later my reaction is a combination of wanting him to kiss me harder while my hand desperately clutches the bedding to stop me from pushing his hand away from my clit. The feelings of having my clit played with while he's still inside me are bringing to a level of orgasm like I've never experienced ever…

~~~

When I finally manage to push his hand away, his dick has gone limp and has slowly slid from my pussy. As it leaves the pussy the tip decides to give me one final taste of heavenly orgasm. It leaves my clit throbbing, hot and with me feeling exhausted in the most languorous way possible.

"I had fun…" I whisper.

"The same. I wish I could do this every day."

"Isn't that possible?" I ask
~~~

"I guess your rule makes it impossible. I wish you'd ignore the rule…"

"I have a plane to catch though. Rule or not."

"I guess I'll have to hope—"

He stops speaking and I glance over to him. I decide not to ask what he hopes for. I'm guessing now that he wants more with me. More than I can give him, even if part of me starts to wonder what's going through his mind. It's like every other guy it seems. First hours of good sex, than the gloom because of the looming separation from me.

"I guess I can decide if you explained it to me. It depends on what you tell me whether I can decide to say yes or no…"

*I hope that sounded sincere enough. Just a perfect flash in the pan way of ruining all this good sex we had really…*

He nods. But he doesn't speak. I'm guessing now that he's considering his options. I just hope one of the options doesn't involve him declaring his undying love for me.

"I guess we need to talk. There are things you need to know. I know you said 'no names' and I'll respect that. But let's make this new rule between us. Just in case we bump into each other in the future, okay?"

He looks at me, and I nod.

"My rule is that every time we *do* see each other that you tell me three things about yourself. You already told me your name is Kitty, so that's one item. Two more and I have my quota for this meeting. I choose what I want to know."

I turn my head and now stare at the ceiling for my own dose of pondering. It sounds fair. I'm guessing I'll get more of this good fucking in return…

"Sure, I can accept the rule," I say, smiling at him warmly. "Make it tempting enough for *me* to want to meet with you, and once you've asked me *three* hundred questions I *want* to answer, you can tell me your name… never before that."

He nods to agree, then suddenly gets up.

# Chapter Seven

"Do you want champagne?" he whispers into my ear after he finally manages to roll over to the other side of the bed. I look at his wide grin, and after a few minutes, I smile at him sensually. I nod. He leaves the bed after soft caress of my nipple followed by a wink.

I watch him go, then after a few minutes, I hear the distinct popping of a cork…

I smile as he walks back into the room and hands me an elegance, part-filled with a sparkle of a sweet-smelling and probably very expensive liquid. I taste and then smile at him appreciatively. He served out the liquid that the hotel probably charges a hundred dollar bill for…per glass.

"So, my sweet darling, are you going to tell me your name?" I ask ever so suggestively. "Or, do I have to go find me another *toy* to play with from your bachelor's party downstairs?"

He smiles at me for a moment. "So, what gave it away that they're there with me for a party?" he asks.

"They seemed so eager to please me when I asked them if you were available…"

He grunts. Of course, he has to grunt. After a pause, he answers. "We could make a deal. I travel for business a lot, and if you want this sort of lifestyle I could arrange it you can travel to anywhere I go for business."

"I can do it. But only if you promise me that you never tell me your name. That would spoil the fun of this…"

I sip from the exquisitely tasting champagne and look at him from the corner of my eye. I know I'm up for the game he proposes. I don't think he realises how tough this is going to be for him.

"Is there a reason why you don't want a name?"

"It's part of the rules. That's all." I shrug my shoulders the lie back flat on the bed, a knowing, sensual smile now dancing on my lips. It wasn't t the first time I've uttered the words.

*I guess I better not tell him about the last few years or else he'll wonder...*

"I guess I can accept the rule..."

I smile when I hear the same hesitation in this man's voice as I've heard so many times before. I guess that I prove every time that the 'guys' can't cope with someone as honest I am. I wait for the inevitable next questions that usually come: "Why the rule? And why no name?"

But to my surprise, he doesn't ask. Smiling sensually I turn my head to look at him. I see him lying beside me, staring pensively at the ceiling.

*I guess playing with me is enough for him. At least for the foreseeable future. But his suggestion...it does offer me opportunities if this is going to be repeated in other places.*

I glance sideways at my prize find. Out of a room of more than thirty men, why did I end up with this man?

"Are you single?" I ask him softly.

A hand lifts up. It shows the faint white on

the ring finger where a ring had been worn. *Not single*, I think with regret, but then I jerk upright when a spoken answer comes.

"I wasn't until three months ago when she decided to cheat on me."

"Oh…how did that happen?" I look at him, smirking somewhat. Guessing that it's interludes like this evening that led *her* to want to favour a different bed.

"I was on a business trip for four months, then got home to find her with him. You met the guy she cheated with downstairs. The guy with the red hair…"

"Oh…right."

I turn my head away, perplexed suddenly at my own feelings. In the greater schemes, I had favoured that guy of this man as a prize find but then something had felt off-putting about him. Like his insincerity could be measured by how much he was smirking at me. In the end, while the red-haired guy had his back turned I grabbed this man by the hand and dragged him to the hotel lobby, then asked to be taken to my room. When he suggested 'fun' in his room at the top of the hotel I was initially wary… that's until the elevator.

"So, about *my* rule…" I begin, turning back to

him and looking into his eyes unflinching.

"If it means I can see you again in the future, I'm fine with it," he answers.

"I cannot make any promises that I'll be there wherever you want to crash with me in…places like this suite. Don't assume I'm a girl that sticks around for one guy."

"I guessed it from the way you eyed the bell boy. It's okay. If you aren't there I guess I'll have another day alone. I'm used to it…"

## Chapter Eight

"WILL YOU TELL ME HOW old *you* are?" he asks. "I know it's usually impolite to ask a girl her age. Just so *you* know, I'll be thirty years old in a few months. When it's my birthday, I'll be on a hot beach and…I'd love it if a hot babe like *you* was lying beside me on the beach… I really would love that. That was also what I was thinking about before I went to get the champagne."

"We'll see…"

"You don't mince your words…" He smirks for a moment. "I guess I can only hope…"

"Is that good or bad? That I'm so blunt. I've chased off guys by being so blunt."

"In your case, it's good. I know exactly where I stand with you. I like you…"

"For a good *fuck*, I guess…"

"More… Why else do you think I want to see you again…?"

"Well, I guessed it was for more fucking me senseless…"

He laughs. Not at me, but for other reasons as it seems. He seems to laugh more at himself for trying so hard with me.

*Why does he want to be with me of all people?*

"The bachelor party isn't for me. If that's the answer you're after…I did overhear your conversation with him. Before you seem to reject him."

"Oh right…so I guess I *can* tell you how old I am. So you know, I'm…twenty-four years old…" I tell him my age, though I curse deep down for sounding so hesitant.

"But I guess that's all I'll find out about you, besides your name… though my rule was three questions."

"I'm sorry. I have my rules…but I guess you can ask me one more question."

"If I can come up with another one, I'll ask it," he says, and then he decides to pause our conversation with a game of playing with one of my nipples.

"Where are you flying to?" he asks. "You mentioned you're waiting for a call about your plane…"

"I'm heading to London…" I answer. "I'm going to see a cabaret show with some of my friends."

"I guess I can't tag along," he says. "Fair enough. Perhaps, one day…"

He turns and grabs his glass of champagne. I do the same, but as I turn away from him I feel a pang of regret. Of *all* prize finds, this guy is possibly the most intriguing one I'd ever found. And of all prize finds he's one I'd want to parade around my friends.

*Perhaps, one day*, my mind echoes the words. But then I realise how insincere the words sound, even to me. *Perhaps, I could go to this beach he mentioned. Perhaps…*

I know my words are more to convince me of the inevitable lack of a 'happy ever after' for him. But I remember being screwed over three years ago by a guy who promised the same, and the rule was there more to stop me getting in the same situation.

I pour all the champagne down my throat,

then I hold my glass out when I see him pour in more for himself. While I sip from my glass I see him drink down three more glasses full.

"I guess I should just finish this damned liquid tonight. The bill for it isn't even mine..." he says, now with a bit of a slur in his voice.

"Whose bill is it then?" I ask.

"The guy with the red hair."

"I guess you can grab the other bottle too then. Serves him right for trying to hit on me when I was only interested in you."

He nods, then adds, "...and for hitting on my ex. Never going to make that mistake again. Revenge will be sweet when his credit card bill comes in. He doesn't even know I rented this penthouse suite when he handed me his card. He said to book whichever room I wanted..."

Once he stops talking I'm laughing hysterically, then I turn on my side, and look at him for a while.

"Okay then, here's an idea. I said that I'd ask your name when you've managed to meet up another ninety-nine times for three questions each. Until that's over my rule is in force. If in those ninety-nine meets you manage to convince me to drop my rule, then you can tell everyone I'm your girlfriend. But..."

"But...?" he asks, and I hear some panic in his voice for the first time.

"...But you cannot tell anyone that until I say it's okay, and you cannot ask me about what I do with my life in the meantime. If *you* convince me, you'll have me for a lot more than just damned good sex...okay?"

"I like the idea. What about coming to the beach on my birthday? And also, like you, I have a plane to catch. I guess I'll have to do it before he discovers what I did..."

"We'll see..." I grin at him teasingly.

"Ah...so you like to tease me. Well then, let's see if you can cope with more good sex right now..."

## Chapter Nine

I'M WOKEN UP BY THE sunlight shining through the cracks of the curtains. I glance sideways and smile when I see him fast asleep. It will make things so much easier...

*No goodbyes...that's part of my rule, too. Except this one will be the hardest of them all. But it has to be done. I hope he'll understand whenever he wakes up and find the bed beside him empty...*

A moment later, I cringe when my cell phone buzzes. I glance at it to see an incoming call. I lift myself from the bed, swooping down for my pile of clothing then dash to the living room.

"Yes…"

I listen to a woman telling me the flight is due for departure in three hours. She explains that check-ins happen at the latest thirty minutes earlier.

*Two hours of boredom left. I guess I have time for a little more fun…*

First, I call my girlfriend in London to let her know when I'm arriving there. I strategically omit the presence of *him* in the bedroom when she asks me what I did to pass the time.

I saunter around the penthouse suite and arrive in a massive kitchen. Glancing around I see a massive clear glass fridge with bottles inside. After opening it I realise this is where the three bottles of champagne had originated from. It seems he'd been drinking more of them before we met in the bar downstairs.

"If that red-haired cheating 'ass' is such a cheater as he has suggested, then maybe I should give him a helping hand in a revenge… My prize find might like it." I murmur.

I grab two bottles and walk with them to the sink. I grin as I pour most of the content into the sink, then after two mouthfuls I place the bottles on the floor beside two others which were obviously placed there by my sleeping 'companion'.

I repeat the action four more times…

I walk to the door of the fridge and look for food. I drink directly from the bottle of orange juice; my brother claims it stops hangovers. Then I grab three of the muffins on a plate next to the fridge. I walk with the juice and muffins to the kitchen table and spend the next fifteen minutes indulging in them.

All the while I eat I listen for the sound of him perhaps waking up, but all I hear coming from the bedroom is the snoring. Not a bother as I grew up with my dad and brother both snoring.

After I finish eating I walk to the shower room, and I take a shower, though being there on my own isn't much fun so I rush with washing. After I'm dried and dressed, I look to the windows to view the vista that I hadn't seen yet.

*He made a good choice taking this penthouse suite,* I

think, smiling now.

After sitting down again at the kitchen table, I decided to write him a letter. It's a new thing. But I want to make it clear to him that I accepted his rule as taken. At the bottom, I write down my voicemail number. If he does decide to take me up on my suggestion of suggesting places to meet, he can send me the details that way so I can find out the details wherever I am and decide on the spot whether I want to go or not…

*I guess time will tell what's going to happen between us. If I do make it to seeing him a ninety-nine more times, and answer all his questions, perhaps I'll have me a proper boyfriend. If ever I were writing a book about this shit, it has to be the next fifty shades, or else…*

I down another few mouthfuls of the juice, then put the bottle back in the fridge. I pick up all my belongings, carrying my shoes in my hands. I can easily walk barefooted downstairs. Just in case…

~~~

As I walk from the bedroom, I glance over one more time at him sleeping in the bed. I have
~~~

another whole day of boredom ahead and for a moment I wish I could take off all my clothes again and rejoin him in bed… He's apparently going to catch his plane later this morning. Where he's flying I don't know. And right now I don't want to know…

*I guess I won't see him again after today. That's okay. There's more meat downstairs to choose from. And he'll know how to contact me if he finds my letter on the table.*

Then I smile as an earlier thought enters my mind, *I wonder if the bellboy is still downstairs. He'll wish he was a virgin by the time I've had my fun with him. I guess I can take him to my room… even if it's just for an hour…*

## The End